Dedicated to the old girls:

Kaloosit, who set the example;

Kati, who gave me this story; and

Canoni, Milakokia, and Ishkoodah,

who pulled it off without a hitch.

Library of Congress Cataloging-in-Publication Data

Powell, Consie.
Old Dog Cora and the Christmas tree / Consie Powell.
p. cm.
Summary: Although Cora has become too old to haul a sled with the
other dogs, she proves that she can still help the family bring in the
Christmas tree from the forest.
ISBN 0-8075-5968-7
1. Sled dogs—Juvenile fiction. [1. Sled dogs—Fiction. 2. Dogs—Fiction.
3. Old age—Fiction. 4. Christmas—Fiction.] I. Title.
PZ10.3.P485501 1999
[E]—dc21   98-53797
CIP / AC

OLD DOG CORA
AND THE CHRISTMAS TREE

Consie Powell

Albert Whitman & Company

Morton Grove, Illinois

Old Cora pawed her dog bed. She had just eaten breakfast and was ready for a nap. She settled down with a sigh.

She had hardly closed her eyes when she heard a commotion in the kitchen. Her daughter and granddaughter were milling around Susan. Cora sniffed the oily scent of leather boots and the sweet smell of well-worn wool. The family was going outside!

Suddenly, Cora wasn't sleepy anymore.

"Come on, girls," Mom called. "Let's put on your harnesses!" The dogs sprang into action.

Ebony danced around the kitchen.

Minx sang for joy.
"Hraa-rhooo!"

Cora gave Susan
a slurpy kiss.

Papa harnessed Minx and Ebony. They followed him outside. Cora waited patiently for her turn.

The oldest harness still hung on the hook. Cora loved that old red harness.

She had worn it to pull Susan when Susan was just a baby.

She had worn it when Minx
and Ebony learned to haul.

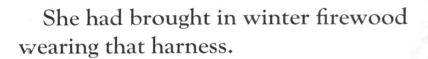

She had brought in winter firewood
wearing that harness.

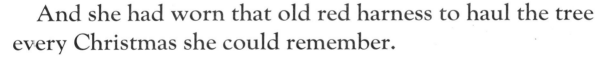

And she had worn that old red harness to haul the tree
every Christmas she could remember.

"Why don't you stay here,
Cora," Mom said. "You're getting
too creaky to pull a heavy load."
    Cora knew there must be a mistake. She never stayed
home when there was work to do. She nuzzled the old red
harness and stared at Susan.

"Mom, we can't leave her behind just because she's too old to pull. You didn't leave *me* home when I was too little to help. Can't she come along just for fun?"

"Okay, Susan." Mom smiled at Cora. "But take it easy, old girl."

Cora glanced at her harness one more time, then followed Susan outside.

Hard-packed snow squeaked underfoot.

Cora wagged her tail as she sniffed the cold December air. A whiff of fox musk floated from the hillside where she used to haul oak logs for firewood. A scent of ruffed grouse came from the clearing where they all picked blueberries in summer. And from the woods on the ridge ahead blew the spicy perfume of balsam fir.

Off the road and into the woods they tromped, looking for just the right tree. Papa wanted it to be tall. Mom insisted it be full. Susan needed it large enough to have extra branches to decorate her room. The dogs didn't care how it looked. They just wanted to pull it.

At last the saw rasped through the trunk of a tall balsam fir. *Whoosh!* Down came the tree! Now it was time for Cora's job.

Papa strapped the tree to the toboggan. Mom called Ebony and Minx and hitched traces from the toboggan to their harnesses. "Susan," she said, "come get Cora. She's in the way."

Susan led Cora aside and fished a dog biscuit from her pocket. Cora crunched it eagerly, then licked her chops. This was all right; someone always had treats when it was time to haul. She asked Susan for another biscuit.

"Okay, girls ... let's go! Hup!" Papa took giant strides, breaking a trail through the deep, fluffy snow. Minx and Ebony tucked their heads, pushed into the padded collars of their harnesses, and followed.

Cora spat out her biscuit and forged past Susan. Something was wrong: they were starting without her!

Cora pushed through the snow to get to
the other dogs. She heard Mom's voice.
"Cora, come back here!" Cora ignored her and
butted in front of Ebony. *Stumble-thumpf!* Cora
toppled forward, tripped by a hidden branch. Minx and
Ebony pushed around her and kept on going.

Cora hurried to catch up with them. She struggled ahead and moved into the trough of pawprints behind Minx. If she could just join the other dogs, everything would be fine. Minx slowed down and her hauling trace drooped. Cora's leg tangled in the slack strap. Everyone stopped.

Papa stomped back to untangle the dogs. "Cora, stay out of the way! You know better than to keep Minx and Ebony from doing their job!"

The rough edge in Papa's voice worried Cora. She was trying hard to do what he had always praised her for doing before. Couldn't he see that?

She stared at Papa for a
moment, then charged into
the woods. She would take
a shortcut through the
aspen thicket and meet
Minx and Ebony up ahead.

Cora had forgotten that she wore no harness. She had only one thing on her mind now: hauling. She remembered the powerful feel of pulling a large tree; she knew how it dragged heavily in the fluffy snow of the deep woods. And she also knew that once they were on the hard-packed road, going would be easier.

Her face dusted with snow, Cora burst from the thicket and squeezed beside Minx and Ebony as they crested the ridge.

Then they were on the road. Minx and Ebony stretched out in an easy lope as the tree glided behind them. Tired but happy, Cora ran next to them. It felt good.

The three dogs trotted steadily, tongues out and tails wagging. But Cora knew where her place was. Nothing could stop her now.

So, in a burst of speed, Cora took the lead.
This was where she really belonged.

"Hey! Look at Cora!" Susan shouted. "She's out in
front!" Mom grinned in amazement, and a smile of
understanding swept across Papa's face.

Eager and joyful, the three dogs covered the last flat quarter-mile with ease. The tree and toboggan coasted to a stop in the yard.

Cora, Minx, and Ebony flopped in the snow, waiting to be unhitched.

Susan got to them first. Cora nuzzled Susan's ear and licked her cheek. "Oh, Cora, you knew, didn't you! You knew you could still do your job!"

Cora sniffed Susan's pocket. Her work was done; now she was ready for a treat.

Papa stooped down to scratch Cora's ears and kissed her on the muzzle. "You *are* a good girl, Cora." Cora swished her tail in agreement.

Mom looked into Cora's deep brown eyes. "Don't you worry, old puppy," she whispered. "Next time, we'll put your harness on you and you can help without being hitched!"

Cora threw Susan a kiss and headed for the back door. Enough hauling for today.

The next time there was a job to be done, she'd be ready.